CHILDREN
~ OF THE ~
GREAT MUSKEG

CHILDREN
OF THE
GREAT MUSKEG

SEAN FERRIS

ACKNOWLEDGEMENTS

I am grateful to those people whose interest and support made this book possible, especially the children of the Great Muskeg; Chief Ernest Rickard and the Moose Band, Moose Factory Indian Reserve; Early Danyluk and the Moosonee Métis & Non-Status Indian Association; Billy Morrison and the Moosonee Native Friendship Centre; the Moosonee and Moose Factory elementary schools; the Weneebaykook group; the Explorations Program of the Canada Council. *Meegwech.*

Published by Black Moss Press, P.O. Box 143, Stn. A, Windsor, Ont. Canada in February 1985. Financial assistance toward this publication was provided by the Canada Council and the Ontario Arts Council.

Black Moss Press books are distributed by Firefly Books, Ltd., 250 Sparks Avenue, Willowdale, Ontario M2H 2S4. All orders should be directed there.

ISBN 0-88753-128-8

Second printing 1991
Printed in Singapore

This book is dedicated to
the people of Moosonee and
Moose Factory Island

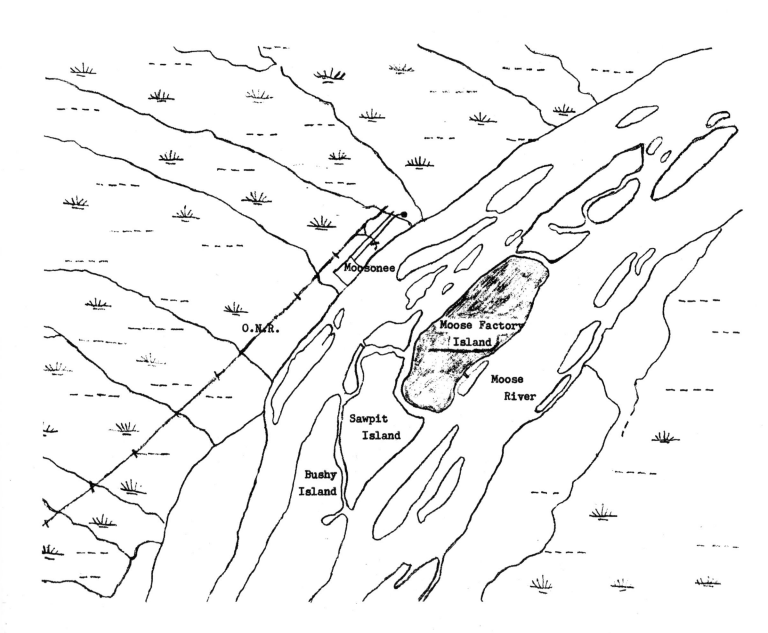

FOREWORD

The Cree and Métis boys and girls living in Moosonee and Moose Factory Island, northern Ontario, are children of the Great Muskeg, that awesome haunted expanse of stunted spruce, tamarack, bogs and fens that is their people's physical and spiritual homeland. The bush hovers at the edges of these rough-and-tumble subarctic settlements on the Moose River and is an elemental force in the children's imaginative lives.

These children are not merely artists, but one does well to focus on their creative energy, because through their drawings, paintings and poems they speak eloquently for themselves about growing up Indian in the Hudson Bay Lowland.

When you experience the powerful images in their work, you enter a world where the people and the earth are of one mind; you smell woodsmoke and hear Canada geese honk their way down the Moose River to the Bay; you shiver in a blizzard before the dreaded Windigo. Your sense of wonder is resurrected and finally you remember what the children know so well — the Great Mystery is all around us and in every moment.

In Moosonee and Moose Factory, where ravens and dogs scavenge muddy roads and winter winds cut to kill, children of the Great Muskeg hunt down their visions and voices and make art that lives.

Sean Ferris

MY STRUGGLE

My struggle is that there is lots of killing
somewhere and I write so messy.
I get homework almost every day when Mr. Rowe
was teaching.
I cry and I try to stop.
I have to work and get up every week till Friday.

MARCELLA TRAPPER, Moose Factory

ME

I am a girl I live in Moose Factory, Ontario
I am an Indian
I like to eat bannock and spaghetti too
I am very happy
I like to play floor hockey
I like to be friends with people
I like to work and help other people
My house is long and wide
I like to clean the house
I like to babysit for my cousins
I like to play video games too
I ride ski-doos around
I like to do art in school because it is fun
And my name is Maureen Blueboy.

MAUREEN BLUEBOY, Moose Factory

ROBERT CHUM, Moose Factory

A STRUGGLE TO LIVE ON MY OWN

A struggle to live — on my own
I have to fight for my home and my life.
I have to live on my own
buy a new house or even build
a log cabin in the bush somewhere.
There are lots of things I have to do,
cut wood for my stove, cook for myself.
I have to find work to make
money for my food, my clothing and my furniture.
Then I can relax after that is all done.

FERLIN DAVEY, Moose Factory

ME — FERLIN DAVEY

Me — Ferlin Davey
I am a boy, a good boy
I go out to see my friends
We play, go see movies —
But we don't fight,
but sometimes we do, but play fight.
I like to dream of having my own house at night.
I like to stay home, read comics, draw
and listen to some rhythm music
I like to ride on my bike in the summer.
I have black hair, brown eyes
I am an Indian
I like to drink tea a lot —
but mom says I have to cut down on it.
Me Ferlin Davey.
I like to eat french fries, but too much, I get sick.
Brian is my best friend, we sleep overnight
at each other's house.
I like to be alone in my room.
I sleep on weekends, in the afternoons.

FERLIN DAVEY, Moose Factory

ME

I am a girl I am 11 years
old. I'm in grade 6. I do
all kinds stuff like work, art,
math, poems. I love doing
poems and I'm doing one now.
I'm lovely, adorable, cute.
I have black hair black eye
balls. I stay on a little, tiny
small Island. It is called Moose
Factory. I also like watching
scary shows like anything.
I'm small, strong, healthy,
moveable, happy, sad and
other kinds of stuff.
I have skinny body skinny
head skinny legs and
other kinds of stuff in my body.

CELINA KATAPATUK, Moose Factory

ME

I am a girl named Laura Trapper
I love my mother, father very much.
I like myself very much
I don't like the teachers
I like animals
I like my friends a lot
I like ice hockey
I like to play outside inside
I like going trapping
I like my house
I don't like school work
I like camping
I like being myself.

LAURA TRAPPER, Moose Factory

PHILIP FLETCHER, Moose Factory

ME, CLIFFORD JEFFRIES

Me, Clifford Jeffries, I'm sometimes mean
and sometimes kind
I like to make people laugh
I like to make them happy
I like it when they make me happy
but sometimes they don't make me happy
that's when I'm mean
I like going hunting
fishing
trapping
but there're times when I can't go
and that's what I hate
and there's people I like
and some I hate
I wish there was
no such thing as HATE
having fun is best of all

CLIFFORD JEFFRIES, Moose Factory

IT WOULD BE BETTER IF...

our ski-doo go slow
our stove works better
our TV work right
our bathroom door's lock
our sleigh does not swing around
if nobody steel ski-doos
broken in houses
if nobody broke windows
if police lock up the drunkers that hang around the store
if nobody shoot around
if nobody have no wars
if nobody steal in the store nobody ride around
when they are drunk
nobody throw garbage around.

KIM LINKLATER, Moose Factory

MY STRUGGLE

My struggle isn't too hard
but I know it's going to get worse
but everyone is going to struggle through
but it's not always easy
when you're young it's easy
when you're old it's hard

CLIFFORD JEFFRIES, Moose Factory

IT WOULD BE BETTER IF....

nobody drank on the Island
we had better roads on the Island
we had a school on the reserve
the world stopped having wars
there were no accidents in the world
people didn't kill each other
I had a bigger bedroom
my mother didn't work so hard
I could go swimming every day
everybody could get a job
there was no garbage lying around on Moose Factory
everybody could go in the bush everyday
there was no tv
there were no cars
there were no ski-doos

BRIAN NOOTCHTAI, Moose Factory

DAVID MARTIN, Moose Factory

IT WOULD BE BETTER IF....

The dishes were done...
My brother would leave me and my sister alone.
The cops picked up drunks...
The garbage put in the cans...
They made a new community hall...
Built better houses in the community...
Made the roads better.
The world was clean and beautiful...
The world had no booze...
The people would take care of the place they live...
The world had no bad people...
The people would love each other.

CHRISTIE ANN FLETCHER, Moose Factory

DAVID MARTIN, Moose Factory

IT WOULD BE BETTER IF....

My bedroom door was fixed.
My house stood at the edge of Moose Factory.
My both brothers don't fight.
My living room lamp works.
My father's car works.
Moose Factory had more police
the kids go home a 9:00
the people didn't drink that lots.
Moose Factory had more stores
the kids had taken no ski-doos
the world had no wars
There was more jobs
There was more schools
There was more houses
There was no killing.

LAURA TRAPPER, Moose Factory

IT WOULD BE BETTER IF....

I helped clean up the house
I didn't lose my cousins pictures
I never say no to my parents
We weren't poor
I start listening to my parents
there would be no stealing
and drinking in the community
there were no bingos
there were no dances
there were no movies
people liked one another
people wouldn't kill each other

I feel funny how the world is.

PAULINE WAPACHEE, Moose Factory

JASON WHISKEYCHAN, Moosonee

DAVID MARTIN, Moose Factory

I AM AN ISLAND

I am an Island
I was a pretty Island
I had flowers growing, birds singing
Everything was perfect until
Man set foot on me
They had machines, trackers, dump trucks
They tore half way through the bush on my Island.
Housing, buildings began to build rapidly
through the Island.
People came, they lived on me
They threw slop, wastes in the dump
My pretty Island was ruined
It's all because of man
The animals and birds had to leave, but the bear stayed.
I am an Island.

FERLIN DAVEY, Moose Factory

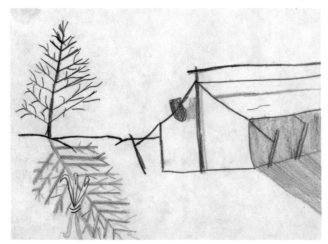

PETER KATAPAYTUK, Moose Factory

DANNY CHEECHOO, Moose Factory

CELINA KATAPAYTUK, Moose Factory

PETER KATAPAYTUK, Moose Factory

Journal excerpt:
   Today I'm going with my father in the bush
to get some wood.

TARA HESTER, Moosonee

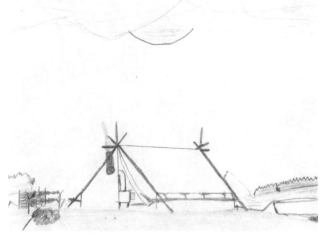

DEREK MOSES, Moose Factory

PETER KATAPAYTUK, Moose Factory

DARREN CHEEZO, Moose Factory

TRINA RICKARD, Moose Factory

DALE CHEECHOO, Moose Factory

CANOEING

going north
going south
going east
going west
I paddle everywhere
going in rivers
having fun paddling down rivers
up rivers
but there's one problem
how do you patch a boat
        Help

CLIFFORD JEFFRIES, Moose Factory

SONNY LOUTTIT, Moose Factory

PHILIP FLETCHER, Moose Factory

CLIFFORD JEFFERIES, Moose Factory

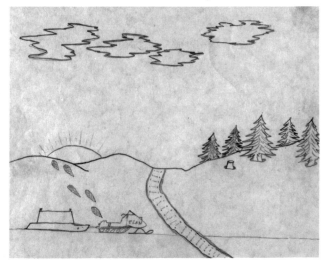

GORDON SACK, Moose Factory

MORNING SUN

The Morning Sun
is always
shining above
    the great
    beautiful
Planet Earth.
       The sun
is like a
    beautiful
big star
   in the
day.
Then at dusk
   it goes
off to another
     Land

PHOEBE SUTHERLAND, Moose Factory

GORDON SACK, Moose Factory

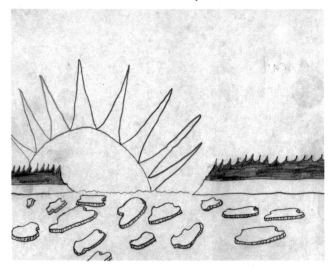

JAMES RICKARD, Moose Factory

UNTITLED

My magic ski-doo
Goes any place
Rum Rum
I'm on my way to the sun.

MICHAEL SUTHERLAND, Moosonee

ROBERT CHUM, Moose Factory

SPRING

Spring is a special season
The bright sun shining all over the place
Geese coming back so you can go hunt
The fresh smell of flowers
The fresh air blowing on your face

DARRELL, Moose Factory

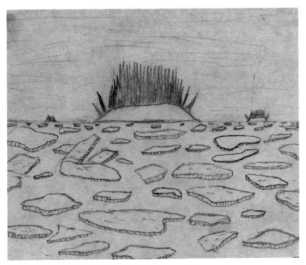

DARRYL CORSTON, Moose Factory

JOURNAL EXCERPTS

I went to Moose Factory to get my pac-man. And I was happy when I got it.

LISA GUNNER, Moosonee

— Last night I was cold. Johnny almost puked. Beht!
— I had a dream
— Last night it was squishy on the bed.

MICHAEL SUTHERLAND, Moosonee

I went to Moose Factory. I had a x-ray. They looked through my skin. They saw my bones.

DARLENE LINKLATER, Moosonee

Yesterday I played outside with Stanley Sutherland. We found a muskrat.

Last night I dreamed my brother was a dog.

SYLVIA MARK, Moosonee

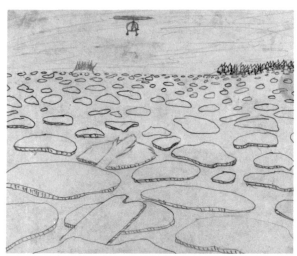

DARRYL CORSTON, Moose Factory

WILLIAM QUACHEGAN, Moose Factory

MY STRUGGLES

I struggle to clean up the house.
To help with the dishes.
I struggle to help me and my friends.
I struggle to start the ski-doo.
I struggle to get along with my brother.
But most of all I struggle to live.

CHRISTIE ANN FLETCHER, Moose Factory

MELINDA WESLEY, Moose Factory

SKIPPING

I like to play
        skipping
      skipping is my
favorite game.
            There are a lot
    of skipping games
              you can play
like ice cream soda, had
            a little
              car,
        Monday night the banjo.
A lot of girls and boys
          play skipping
          at school.

CARLENE LOUTTIT, Moose Factory

MY STRUGGLE

My struggle is very tough
the boys on this Island
sure make it tough
I roam around to find
a friend
but I always
wind up alone again
try as I might
I never find one right
but I just might find one,
and we'll play
and have fun.

CHRIS FARIES, Moose Factory

ROBERT CHUM, Moose Factory

MY STRUGGLES

I sleep the way I want to
I fight the way I want it.
I cry when I want to cry
I work every day in school and I try my hardest.
I print and write and I get some homework
and I sit beside my friend Marcella Trapper.
I get some friends
I have fun too.
I do a lot of stuff in Moose Factory.

MAUREEN BLUEBOY, Moose Factory

FRIENDS

Friends can be good or bad
Don't ever help your friends if they are bad
Find a friend that is nice and good
Take her away with your family
Be good to her
You can give her a gift
Give her something pretty
You play with her today
run run be a good friend to her
After the day is finished tell her goodbye
We can be friends forever.

KIM LINKLATER, Moose Factory

UNTITLED

Beavers are in danger. The splash me in the face.
I cry when they splash me. They try to drown me. My friend
Bullfrog saves me. We got married.

MICHAEL SUTHERLAND, Moosonee

WYNONA CHEECHOO, Moose Factory

THE GLOBER

The Glober smashed Tronto
it killed all the people in
Tronto it left nothing
but ashes

AUTHOR UNKNOWN, Moose Factory

MY BALLOON

My balloon is taking me to
a place called
Hollywood. I see Shirley Temple
and some other
stars, it's wonderful and
exciting. I see a mean
looking man he chases
me and he busts my
balloon, I start to cry I
was very sad. I had no way
to go home.

CARRIE WAPACHEE, Moose Factory

THE DRAGON

I wish I had a dragon. He could take me to the desert
and I could look at snakes and lizards then go home. At
night I sneek out the window and call my dragon and go
back to the desert and look at the snakes and lizards
sleep. Then I head back home and go to sleep.

DARRELL WHISKEYCHAN, Moosonee

PLANET OF THE SKUNKS

Once upon a time I said to myself, I guess I should go to
the planet Mechebula. So I did. I went by my pet dragon.
I let it out of its cage. It flew around. I said, come here.
It did and I said to him, go to planet Mechebula. I got on
top of its tail. Then we landed there. I got off it. Then I
looked around.

I saw lots of skunks. I saw the king after. The king
said get him. I ran away. The king's name was Evil
Skunk. The king said come here. I said No. The skunk
came after me. I got my gun out. I shot some. The
skunks sprayed at me. I got my shield out. Their spray
was gas. I got my mask on.

When the gas went away, I shot some again and that
was it. I shot the king. Then I got on my dragon. Then
we went home. That night I had a dream about the
skunks.

LEROY QUACHEGAN, Moosonee

ANDREW WHISKEYCHAN, Moose Factory

THE LITTLE BOY AND HIS FATHER

Once upon a time there was a boy who lived with his father. The boy's name was James. He had a bowandarrow. He liked to shoot animals. His father liked him. His father had a gun. One night Indians came in. They came bardging in the house. James got up and got his bowandarrows. James went to get his father. James father was going to shoot one of the Indians. One of the Indians shot James father. James father died after. They took James away. Later James had an Amonia. When James had Amonia he die too. All the Indians die too. The End.

ROBERT ETHERINGTON, Moosonee

WAYNE TOMATUK, Moose Factory

MY TALL TALE

One day I went under my blankets and there was a
rocket and an elf was there.

   He told me to come in but I was too big and he said
some magic words and I went small.

   Then we took off and he said we are going into a
magic world and we saw an orange goose in space.

NELSON CHEECHOO, Moosonee

TONY McDONALD, Moosonee

ARTIST UNKNOWN, Moose Factory

SYLVIA MARK, Moosonee

WINDIGO

Hair like burnt moose moss
Head like a meat ball
Eyes like burning red ashes
Nose like a pig nose
Mouth like a flaming red hoop
Lips like red circles
Voice like an angry moose call
Breath like the dump
Teeth like sharpened swords
Ears like potatoes
Neck like a bear's neck
Body like a giant
Heart like all iceberg
Arms like stretchy telephone wires
Hands like bears' claws
Legs like ice tunnels
Feet like weiners
Toes like sliced apples

SYLVIA MARK, Moosonee

DALE CHEECHOO, Moose Factory

BARBARA CHUM, Moose Factory

40

PAUL McLEOD, Moose Factory

IAN ARCHIBALD, Moosonee

43

CHERILYN WESLEY, Moosonee

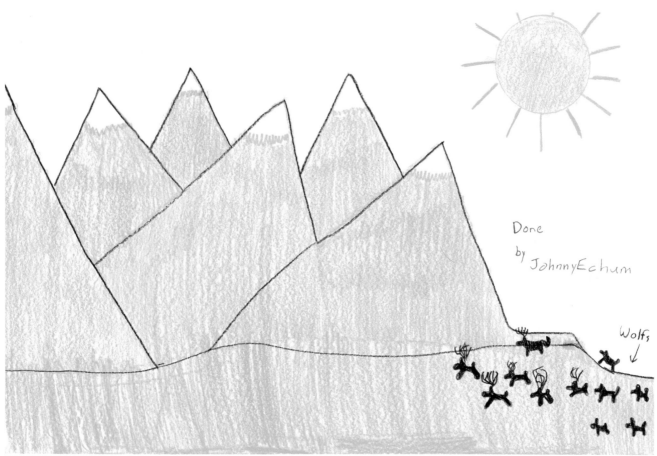

Done
by JohnnyEchum

Wolfs

JOHNNY ECHUM, , Moose Factory

45

PAUL McLEOD, Moose Factory

QUENTIN CHEECHOO, Moose Factory

VERNA, Moose Factory

KEN CHUM, Moose Factory

DAVID MARTIN, Moose Factory

FROG

In yesterday I was going to somebody's house. When the kids saw a frog. It was jumping. So I pick him or her up. So she was very happy. So I went to get the water. So I saw her swimming. And see me too. When she was almost died I let her go at water. So at last time she was gone now. So I like the frogs. And I didn't kill the frog. So at that time I was going home. And think about the very nicest frog pet.

ERNEST CHOOKOMOOLIN, Moosonee

A WILD BEAR AND HER CUBS

A wild bear and her
    cubs were in
    our house it was
in the afternoon
  on
    Saturday
  she tore down
 the chairs and
broke the dishes
    and cups
        because someone
        stole her cubs

DIANE JOLLY, Moose Factory

ARTIST UNKNOWN, Moose Factory

WHERE WILD WINDS BLEW

Where wild winds blew,
to and fro
Where wild animals roamed,
there was a great wild prairie,
long long ago.

JEANNE CHABOT, Moose Factory

HORSES

Horses are fast as the wind,
        they run faster than
you can.
People love to ride
        them almost every
moment.
I would say horses
are the nicest in the
        heart!

CARRIE WAPACHEE, Moose Factory

WINIFRED KATAPATUK, Moose Factory

AUTUMN IS

Golden leaves
    all around
you
    you
      can hear
    the cry
      of the
    North Wind
      and
the wolf's
    cry for
    food

PHOEBE SUTHERLAND, Moose Factory

COLIN MacDONALD, Moose Factory

JACK RICKARD, Moose Factory

JACK RICKARD, Moose Factory

WILLIE SMALL, Moose Factory

THE MOOSE

The moose is out in
the dark cold marsh.
The white man comes to kill it
without praying to the moose.
The moose knows that man has come.
For the man came from
the north side when
the wind blows to the moose.
The moose gets up from
his dreary sleep he smells the
scent of the white man.
The moose gets up in fear and
runs for his life he knows
the man has a gun.

MARINA BUTTERFLY, Moose Factory

DAVID MARTIN, Moose Factory

KEVIN ETHERINGTON, Moosonee

RAVENS

Sneaky
        Squawky
Big
    Black
        Birds
Very
    Special
        Ravens

PATRICK LINKLATER, Moosonee

MICHAEL TOOKATE, Moosonee

PHILIP SUTHERLAND, Moose Factory

THE BIRD

If I was a bird I would fly high in the air just for you
And I would count all the waves just for you
I would fly around the world just for you
I would soar in the forest and I would do
all these things for you

CLINTON McLEOD, Moose Factory

DARRELL CORSTON, Moose Factory

IF I WERE A GOSLING

When I was born I took my first big step. I tumbled down the hard willows. Then I saw the water. I took one step in the water. Right away I knew that I was swimming. The first problem I ran into was a snapping turtle then a snake. Then I called my mother. She hissed and scared it away. She hit me back to the nest. I felt sad when she got mad at me.

LISA CORSTON, Moose Factory

SONNY LOUTTIT, Moose Factory

DARRELL CORSTON, Moose Factory

WAYNE TOMATUK, Moose Factory

TONY MacDONALD, Moosonee

ROBERT CHUM, Moose Factory

MICHAEL SUTHERLAND, Moosonee

WILLIE SMALL, Moose Factory

WILLIE SMALL, Moose Factory

GLEN CHUM, Moose Factory

TODD ROACH, Moose Factory

WILLIE SMALL, Moose Factory

GLEN CHUM, Moose Factory

PAUL McLEOD, Moose Factory

MICHAEL SUTHERLAND, Moosonee

PHILIP FLETCHER, Moose Factory

JOHN ETHERINGTON, Moosonee

DONNY MARTIN, Moose Factory

INDIANS

Tall, Muscular
Hunting, Trapping, Running
Indians are really strong
Indians

KAREN SACK, Moose Factory

ROBERT CHUM, Moose Factory

EDWARD HARDISTY, Moose Factory

TRAPPING

Trapping is a native culture
Remember when Indians went trapping for a living
Always they would come back with something
People nowadays go trapping very seldom
People trap for beaver, rabbits and other animals
Indians respect the animals
Natives a long time ago thanked the gods when trapping
Going trapping is great!

LILLIAN SMALLBOY, Moose Factory

JIMMY WAPACHEE, Moose Factory

NISKA

The niska flies southward in the northern sky.
The large old sun sets itself among the wildly grown trees.
The niska fly in a way so they could trick the hunters.
But the hunters make blinds out of branches, weeds and
other things.
The sit and wait for the niska that is so precious to the Cree
people.
Hunters go home with geese for the whole family.
This bird is the most life-giving bird in the Moosonee
district.

MARY WABANO, Moosonee

STEVEN CHUM, Moose Factory

DONDUS WEAPENICAPPO, Moose Factory

71

PHILIP BLACKNED, Moose Factory

UNTITLED

My name is Nelson Cheechoo. My hobby is drawing.
My favourite sports are football and swimming.
I was born in Moose Factory. Every fall and spring
people from Moosonee and Moose Factory go hunting
for geese and moose. My favourite TV shows are
Dukes of Hazzard, Battlestar Galactica, Star Wars
and Incredible Hulk.

When I went hunting I was using a 4-10 and I almost
shot a goose but I missed. But we got 13.

NELSON CHEECHOO, Moosonee

GOOSE HUNTING

When the geese start
flying, the men would go and
kill the geese.
The women would pluck
the geese
and then they clean the
geese.
After, they cook the geese.
Boy does it ever taste
good.

JENNIFER SUTHERLAND, Moose Factory

DARRELL CORSTON, Moose Factory

SONNY LOUTTIT, Moose Factory

CHERYL RICKARD, Moose Factory

WINTER SEEN

And there it was
black it could match the snow
or not
I screamed 'cause it
didn't match the snow
My mother was alive and
dead
that was my mother
Who matched the snow
her name is snow beast

PAULINE WAPACHEE, Moose Factory

JOURNAL EXCERPT:

Last night I went to the movie.
The world's best medicine man
wanted to get born again.

LEROY QUACHEGAN, Moosonee

CARMEN DAVEY, Moosonee

JOURNAL EXCERPT:

I dreamed that a Dracula tried to get me.
I ran and I ran in the bush and he got me.
And I got scared and I woke up.

JOHN SACKANEY, JR., Moosonee

WINDIGO

Hair like black skinny wieners — and fuzzy
Head like a black and red snowball
Stitched-up eyes
Nose like a red fireball
Mouth like a warty and bloody thing
A deep and loud voice
Smelly and stinky breath
Teeth like sharp yellow knives
Big monkey ears
Neck like a wire
Heart cold as ice
Grizzly bear hands
Feet like Rupert House canoes

VALERIE CAREY, Moosonee

WINDIGO

Hair like a mop
Head like a wolf
Eye like a red ball
Nose like a person's
Lips like a big E
Voice like a horn but hundred times louder
Breath like a garlic — his breath could kill you
Teeth like a tiger
Ears like a wolf
Neck like a skinny
Body like a person's
Heart like a rock
Arms like a monkey
Hands like a bear
Legs like a person's
Feet like a canoe
Toes like a shape of a claw
Face like a scab

CARMEN DAVEY, Moosonee

RICKY CRAWFORD, Moosonee

NATURE

Then, it was beautiful and unspoiled,
the animals roamed free with no fear,
they were the friends and were content,
but then something happened,
a new person came, the white man.
He brought with him the guns, the people.
He destroyed the old world for something new.
And now look what has happened.
Many animals are gone, they're history.
The beautiful landscape has now turned into
a noisy, loud place to be with no room to think.
Why should we be proud of the world
when it has destroyed us — the Indian people!

VALERIE ISERHOFF, Moosonee

MUSKEG AND ME

Here I am walking
Walking in my moccasins
Walking on you the Muskeg
You are so wet and cold
So quiet and cold
And as I walk on you
You say to me
Let me guide you
To a place where you and others will go
In a place where there's peace and solitude

FRANCES FOX, Moosonee

DAVID MARTIN, Moose Factory

TONY MacDONALD, Moosonee

THE INDIAN

Upon a hill, a man stands
His long hair flowing free

On a street, a man flounders
Lost in an unknown world

Once the same two people
but now two different minds
One for the past another
for the present.

What has happened to
the Indian?

Before he roamed the
plains so free
but now he's lost
on a city street.

I guess it was once
upon a time.

ANITA ETHERINGTON, Moosonee

WILLIE SMALL, Moose Factory

WILLIE SMALL, Moose Factory

OUR LAND

We were first, we the red people,
Our Land was green, pure and clean
No sound of anything at all
Except for birds singing on tall trees
Buffalo thundering across the prairies
Bear eating and sleeping in the great wilderness
Fish swimming up and down the streams
and rivers and our great Oceans
But today you came along you white people
Our Land, our animals, were our friends
Our perfect friendship is all gone.

FRANCES FOX, Moosonee

WILLARD VINCENT, Moose Factory

DARRELL CORSTON, Moose Factory

THE BEAT OF MY FATHER'S DRUM

Sitting around an open fire in the woods.
Looking deep into the fire I can see my
great ancestors dancing, drumming and offering
thanks to the great Gitché Manito.
As the fire cracks the burning wood
I can hear the distant beat of my father's drum.
As the birds sing I can hear the singing
of my people
then as I look around me there are all
kinds of people.
I feel that I don't belong to this clan.
I feel the urge to change the world to
how it was many, many moons ago.

MARY WABANO, Moosonee